Love And Wine

And

Wide angle lens

Evincepub Publishing

Evincepub Publishing

Parijat Extension, Bilaspur, Chhattisgarh 495001
First Published By Evincepub Publishing 2020
Copyright © Partha Chakraborti 2020
All Rights Reserved.

ISBN: 978-93-90362-69-1

LOVE AND WINE

AND

WIDE ANGLE LENS

BY

PARTHA CHAKRABORTI

"This book is dedicated to my Parents who are no more"

Preface

This book is a double book
and a book of contrast.
It has two parts.
Purely for pecuniary reason.

First part " Love and Wine " are lyrical love poems written
when I was young.

Second part "Wide angle Lens" is prose poetry, free verse
with lyric plots and prose plots interchanged and cerebral.

It searches many shades of life.
It requires slow and intense reading.

The words that we often write we do not seek to mean.
Loving someone is not same as desiring which is hormonal
and sensory. Imagining the absurd and abstract against
diurnal routine requires
metamorphosis of the self.

It is the heart of this book.

Most writer pen things because of passion. Feelings floats
beyond
boundary and depth of words.

That makes description partial, but I walk the trap while
searching allure of light.

Rocketing friendship with the elusive
is a never ending journey.

I may fail miserably because I seek change.

That is no deterrence. Because any art progresses through
creative destruction.

If my symphony touches a single soul that will count as
reward.
Readers are protagonist in my journey.
I need your light to remove
darkness from within.

'Simplicity is Cocaine'

can see....
god's spine is broken

-Partha Chakraborti

Contents

Love And Wine

WIDE ANGLE LENS

Ballad of Blood

I am the summer
that born in pain

I am the summer
that look for the rain

I am the rain
that look for the tree

I am the rain
that make thirsty free

I am the wind
that wish you close

I am the fire
that give you rose

I am the autumn
that stay naked

I am the winter
that look jaded

I am the love
that flame the storm

I am the heart
where you blossom

I am the spring
spray love with colour

I am the love
and you my desire

Pin my heart
my blood be
on your feet

Cut my flesh
and I will give you
fleshy treat

Break my leg
my hand will hold
you like flower

Cut my throat
I will die once
But willing to die

A thousand times
and say
" I love you forever ".

Glow

Hurt me....

I will pass
like a flow...

Fall
as snow.....

I will make
you..

Silky Glow..

Fire Song

You bled my lips
   passion raged
but where is
   your soul

You raised waves
   in my naked body
but no caress
   only hands crawl

You pushed me hard
   harder than hammer
but never touch me soft
   where is your heart

   "O dear "

You lifted me high
   with coated words
top of a ivory tower
   made love beside clouds
but, shards everywhere ....

It is always
   like this
you pretend
   you are near

My heart spins
for you
but you are
not there

For how does the
soul works
No matter where the
bodies are

Why do you say
you love me
while your heart
is not on Fire.....

Bleed

She came to
Bleed me

.....departed

I became two

... one consoled
the other

Until I became
water....

I don't loose
blood anymore.

Murmur

Mind and fingers
in symphony...

Removing last piece
from your body
desire and surprise awaits
to feel you with you...

I kept my ear
slowly in your chest
to hear whisper of...soul...

Boundary of desire broken...

Unconceived you...emerges
from infinite depth...

murmur.........

.........outside is just a
shadow of you's.....you

The invisible Whole.....

Winey

Real muse
is a rainbow

She wears
Fire and water

Morning,
She gives
you raindrop.....

At.. night,
Winey lips,
Curvy flames.. encounter

She may look
as flower
Inside
infinitely deep.....

Love her madly
Else don't
make the trip....

Madness

In her madness
there is sparkle
when she is weird
she is deep

Gently dive to
find the mystery...

Smile

Between sensuality
and spirituality
with wing
she flies

wild,
fear...her wildness
the sun
never tries

the moon
dare to
bath her......,
the rose
stay wise

the storm stops
on her way
the moment
she smiles.........

Wings

He cheated her
And took someone
Else's hand

She lost faith
In love
An innercall
An angel came

Don't worry
My girl
How long
You will keep
Folding your wings

And, she fluttered her span
And fly up high
To be free....Again

Offer

Where is the promise that
Sun will burn forever
Where is the promise that
Life will always be fare....

Where is the promise that
Love is permanent
and
Heart will beat..forever.....

As long as...it burns or,
As long as....
It beats....

Smell....time
for an experience
Hard to gather.......

Give love a soft chance,
even if nobody cares...

Life is.....bizarre,
desert of selfishness

Why not fake
It's nature's best offer.

Difference

Men are
born with wings
fly..up and up
....until they fall

Women are rivers
deep deep ......river..

where she is
where she will be
....no one knows............

Wonder

God has created
  two wonders
  universe
  and woman

The first is
  infinity
The second is
  life.

She makes
  everything bigger

If you give vegetable
  she will produce
  delicious dishes

If you give her love
  she will give family
If you give house
  she will make home

*If you give respect
  she will create legacy*

Miracle

With five elements
and little bit of magic
we emerge.

Then every moment is
a miracle of life.
It unfurls on the edge
making rich experience
of glass.

Then oneday,
we go home
to be dust again.

Attachment

My soul
my body
are without bindings

I never confuse
romantic love, lust and,
long term attachment

Each runs it's course
until the last one
acquire spine

The first and second
have wings.

Burning

In her chaos
there is beauty.

Treat her tenderly
as wild flavour ....

Because butterfly
never knows
how beautiful she is.

She will know
in her flame
you are burning
your life....and desire...

Soul ' O ' soul

Is it dreamland
laced in ecstasy

Is this moonlight
appear before dusk

Is it oneness like mercury
shape unchanged
with thousand cut

Is it that illusion
where dream
mirror's reality

Is it déjàvu that
fuses two soul

But I am looking for earthly love
and friendship
in this lifetime with you..

Important

Who is most
important in life....

You think,
 I am talking love.

I am talking
 about myself

Only one person
  is deeper than ocean
  heart larger than sun.

Mother...
she gives her life
the greatest warrior
for your life
who protects and soothe you
when pain kill
the soul.

Miss

Human are not flowers
There could be beautiful face
with a envied mind

It's multitude without anchor.
So in love there could be sky
and abyss.
But not taking the risk
will be the biggest miss.

Dream

President Kalam said
Dream is not what
you see in sleep......
But what keeps you
awake at night.

I disagree
had that been the case
Shahjahan would have been
The greatest emperor
for Tajmahal....

Material

What an enigma....
We all are Traders.

Everyday we sell
our minutes of life
to acquire materials
even though,

We have to leave
our body here..........

Silent Durga

They say all women
   are " Durga".
   Shakti..
   conquers
   all negativities

I wanted to become
   your support, strength

When you down and out
   I wanted to give shoulder
   where you can lay head

I will collect all your pain
   hide inside my heart
   free you from it's rain

I wanted to be like a
   banyan tree
   give you shadow
   and resting place

I just wanted to be
   beside you
   as a partner in
   strength and sorrow

I wanted to be beside you
for struggle and glory
as " Silent Durga "
today or tomorrow

Mannequin

Feel her lips
with the fire
of your soul..

in the chaos
you bet all...

she will know
you...are
"the man".....

not a
part timer
mannequin

but a flaming
scintillating champagne......

Hiroshima

Madness
in love
is gasoline....

when
meets
with eccentricity
it burns like
Hiroshima.........

Genius

In love
no one is genius..

Like the dews
of winter
slowly sinks....

The heart
in her thought
slowly fills

With time
soul on fire....

The world
is she ..
The heat
blows everywhere.....

Orange

We look for
music.....

who has everything..........

To me
a broken love

Blooms...... Orange

Sonata

My secret thoughts
are draping you
My melting soul
is sculpting you...

Prada's
Dream lingerie
cannot match
your wild eyes...

With fire
you put moon
in shame..

As it cannot
outsoothe you
in tenderness game

You are only you
in life's wild
reference frame...

You are...only you
Heaven's...Dame.

Simple Things

You always loved
  flashy cars
  whizzing at
  180 km per hour

Big flat glass top
  so that you can
  see rain and blue sky

You loved parties and
  wild events
  late nights

I adjusted and adjusted
  You never asked
  what I look for

Simple things that stitch
  two souls

I never wanted Rolls Royce
  you just value me
  and my voice

My needs are daily calls
  You catch me
  when I fall

WIDE ANGLE LENS

Wide angle lens

At the edge of convention you think
political economy rescued the deserted.

You are a rising wave suspended halfway
spinning in aura of expectation.

Extreme inequality, poverty,
failed systems advancement, mass fragmentation
a political curiosity.

That's exactly a geometrical loop
on which your sexual irony lies.

The automatic ignition of the spacecraft smeared a large
cloud of powder
from the exhaust whose contents
absorbed cortex in your grey.

The cold rationale just bonded the nucleotides without
phosphate sugar chain...

If the house is half white in moonlight
your highbrow will be thawed at the junction intersecting
angular momentum of thought and dispersion of reasoning
and neural correlate that heightens perceptions.

So in the car when you are exposed to your secretary's
provocative hemline,
you uncompromised your masochistic urge at the
emergence
of my face.

That's a unilateral confession
...your vapid defence.

On the big house of greenfield,
the carpet need to be stitched with air and vanilla and you
dropped the idea of Persian culinary to bring a sober end
of
Russian roulette for selecting Mexican dishes for dinner.

And in your late venturing into painting using cloud colour
in space canvass bringing

"Dream within a dream"
appears celluloidal replica of
Duchamps "Monalisa", L.H.O.O. Q.

" There is fire below ".

And you abandoned engineering for researching a new
project

"Intrigue in love of women and man for fucking" even when
they are not far from grave.

Life to you a game of sincerity where you hold the other
end to tug a bull that remained unfed for days and you have
a job that whistle you to the sky when it sees red.

It's mid-summer,
experience of frustration all around until cloud becomes
cold and liquid and cannot store anymore, spills soft
diamond crystals to keep sensorial cold amid humid high.

And you want to hypnotize one god
put your record straight to seek clarity on the status of
mankind, enlighten humanity to seek the most powerful
like
SunGod of "Akenaten".
Eventually that turned into dew
faded from posterity.

What turned then ?

"style and subjectivity " disappeared,
you enamoured with structure and form
while cognition stumble,
You plan to capture objective absurdity in radiofrequency
mode without filling cognition's imprint between
"absurdity and illogicality"
in colour with form, structure, words using motor
generating no impulse.

Some aesthetics cannot be unfolded and experimented in
canvas of mind let alone in Perspex.

Your benevolence in uncertainty a thrill.

Your cock lifted, ready without face, place and time as your
honesty and poise.

It never fathoms your grey and soul at the climax of high
configuration.

And you are unaware that you cannot smell abyss but fail
to be wide.

 You think as a protagonist for this outré,
 will eventually outshine all idea.

As a record of arrogance you forget humility in creation
So the depth unfounded.

*Every innovation eventually reverts to banality mimicking where
sensing beauty is froth.*

Pain is fractional panacea
clean error and dirt of mind from soul.

You use experience and light to discover ever changing
horizon in solid cloud.

Sensing bodily, mentally, mystically socially and in divine
form is a supernatural polyphony
beyond your cognition.

You are happy in this earthly confidence.

And that abhors your meteoric speed.

How arbitrariness, form, colour, words
and sense of causality interacts in creating shape in
complex
plane of retro causality in a regression to justify the
plurality in enquired wisdom where branches and subparts
are in non conformity, floats unsettled in the webby
loop in four dimensional net,
is still a blackbox for the most.

Eventually,
mysterious problem is more mysterious on the waterfront.

You hate arbitrariness and paint words as
melody with praise,

Colour duration on someone's mental plane to capture
physicality.. and that's your default error

Need reprogramming not rebooting.

So that's the fate and you lovingly kill the language
and you realize it's far from enough....

There is a difference between buying sex and love's
wholesomeness in temporality.
Love is a pseudo construct not outside

the biological boundary where entire consciousness
becomes bodily sex organ
for orgasm.

You confident in this art, looking for highest peak on the
masochistic Richter scale which coincide with nervy
drumbeat.

And you believe that's life best reward,
yet that's pastiche.

You still believe grandeur, foppiness world is imprisoned
in big house, wealth property, status and power that elite
cornered is substantive.

Your everything is a rational construct in a time arrow
independent of civilization 's momentum meeting
crosscurrents of political and philosophical smoke.

Injecting neutral characters like a chair
or basin in a room in your canvas cannot remove the irony
of idea.

Your neural network starve for new input. Yet output
devours energy.

So with time a kind of inchoate and spasmic aberrations
evolves in bubbles in the flow, in your thought
that art and artist, poet and poetries can be out of sync
quiet easily

in the apparently chaotic but routined
life.

If taxonomy is foam in rapidly shifting
surface your confidence fumbled.

Sometime you have to see men not a as
reassemble of dust.. but a spine upright.

Truthfully without grumble and grudge.

Come straight,
what you see in unfolding life,
your future and that can unsettle your
imagined surface.

Come out of pleasurable high tide of beauty engulfs your
periphery.

Halt like camera your visual motors and take a deep breath
and look at the world outside each item.

All static form
expand your sexual sensorium
imagine with closed eye without memory recall...the
unimaginable

That splits your cognition to imagined and abstract world
the gap arises...that's poetic art
which is real.

Will this clue be enough ?
You need more ?
Add and delete more or
the delta of change will be inappropriate.

Think breasts
Think castration
Think void
Think orchard
..........Anything,

Remove layer by layer of reality...

Can you do this in progression without words, colours or
thought to a volatile abstract.

Let's visit a lake or a park.
Sit down.

Slowly remove belief of an idea

Remove belief of absurdity

Halt perception in conclusion's arrow

Perceive fucking as neutral act

God as a tragedy of mankind

Avoid revolution's trap

Delete life's banality and salvation

Just expand the circle of sensorium.

You are indoctrinated by your shadow in half sleep and
perception
It becomes misty at the edge of senses.

Now I understand your corpus, the unfathomable with
superposition.

The representation of the problem is partly undefined and
curiosities crosscurrents can give any name
yet the problem is unbloomed in the grey.

Let life kick your "pleasure can" down the road in fleeting
syllables with gaps muse code undeciphered and locked.

The roadside narrative is all
Your past present and future.

Kolkata Tune

Drum beats of silence in deep black, before dawn, stroll
near Hooghly river,

Dews arrow perforate, dried salty nerve ends fire the
neurons with cold smells.

Crows one by one gathering, to eat the leftover offerings,
departed gaping, floating between hell and heaven,
pretlok.....

Sudden blast of hooked silencer of a launch's clunky
engine begins the beginning.

The serpentine web of kolkata,
Life slumbered, entering slow crawl back,
Lass and lads in pool cars,

Schools, torture out routine's history,
Time curvy, tea stalls lifting shutters,
A classical tune moist the golden flow,
Pandit's finger stroke resonate Ramshackled house, where
on top, a banyan tree kisses the orange of first hope.

I remember, your raw lips, but then, that was a different
you.

Now, Mother Ganga, awed, city has more heights, more led filled Rabindra Sadan, Torned jeans, lovers and Baul singers with guitar, dotara improvised, mixed genres...jamming.

Do your lips kept that magic, still gasping, bombarded by dotted cells, carrying memories of first electricity.

Now...rainbows are rare, pollutants clouded city's lungs...wizards gone underground and all those grass, our witness to eternity, replaced by concrete and the pointer, flashes at roads denounce in acrimony, the mutation of that warm kiss by a genetic spear, changed space...time.

That stammerer, hotel waiter's smile advanced, for tips, now, don't know the skin's ridges, lost shines with grey on the hair, that walked the time, I still roll, sniffing...those spots.

The daily circle of congruence is now widely locked straight line.

If ever, memory flashes your unconscious, draw a circle...I am the centre remembering and whetting the scattered ..you pause and reflect and erase the dot before we turn ashes...while new symphony plays for another one for another tomorrow.

On earth briefly romancing life

Life facing life
Middle of a
Seven road Crossing........
Park Circus

Choices many
I have no plan

Cars go all the way
So did men
Like spider
sitting on a web

All roads enigma
conscience
Still uncertain.....

Others driven to need
Walking
wearing curtain

Through every road
I can go anywhere
but not to the heaven

The dewed grasses
have a mystical call....

Can be to Garer Math
But no dense forest
where outcomes
meets the time

All are asphalt walks
where time sloths
Life is broken circle
Routine is downfall

Don't want any
praised existence of rose.

For it knows
sticking to death
on a branch for life
not a matter
of applause.

I wished a life
that give pain
and flashes surprise

Will not see number
the first bus
arrives

I will ride
and be lost

in a land where
grasses dance

Beetle speaks tales
sparrows laugh
Silky moon sings soprano
no one wails.....
no rise or fall graph

Life is life
and no race
where one go.....

I walked
the unwalked
whether
wonder or pain flow

Can share this
with all.....
where soul glow

Death..Arrives
without a plan and
can take me untidily

Halfway....

Led a life
by becoming unkind to myself

never wanted to miss a surprise
or the unseen
wandering beyond daily grudges

Missed few sketches
in horizon
with little regrets

Beyond rainbow
I straddled
heart flied on wings

Tearing strings of attachment
I fell in this ocean
to listen the music
as child unwise.

Gate in heaven's Corridor

One day, I entered a museum full of
mirrors with no reflections.

One chamber, the stars serving caviar,
Other a flying python drinking champagne.

A walking bat befriended a jellyfish enjoying moonwalk in
a square grassland beside the junction of a valley full of
edelweiss and cloud.

A lawn of snow floating mid-air,
talking to a hill about slivery lake
that produces rosewater that shines in darkness.

A doctor treating a madman on the
top of a tricycle with a injection of wine to open his close
mind.

Finally, a pair of lovers exchanging kisses with a bee that
stings their emotions and grab tears to fill the hive.

Now, earth's shadow float in the mid-air.

I talk to the cloud....fulfil one desire, to have the smell and
touch of falling Kohinoor on my forehead from electric
cloud and smell heaven, before death comes
for assessment and fix the date.

The journey, where so many truths allure,
darkness opens the door, offer the throne
...as dishonesty bloomed it's life.

Among the doer of injustice
who were snaked in to live for eternity
with curse by the lawmakers of karma, I
find Gods of society corrupted filled hell
and drinking red.

I float in this symphony with a cigar in hand, burning
furiously without smoke.

Morning dews are liquid diamonds
with innuendo,

Ready to show heart
where everyone is a book
and pages are open for a walk
in half dark.

That's how it bloom

That's how it bloom.

An idea like a stone evolved in seafloor with fins and tails,
the high tide catch the moon and sunlight for a while,
became froth and bite the bullets on
the way to create a recipe inside.

Someone always picked up the sword to conquer different
land, inserted libraries of his greatness. Someone else,
questioned inconsistencies, became anthropological in
accumulating evidences.

Research is an action of evolution with revolution as half
brother. Quagmire lifted in the new chapter blocked
someone's plot. And distributes the unsettled deep blues
magic as ubiquitous but half understood which drag me
too, in the complexity of slow rise from the bottom to
people's movement. I like many, unfigured part of the plot
and rest of the scaled motive.

And I woke up last night in a dream,

Flying over a ruin, a lost civilization, people reappeared
and buzzing, invited me for a dinner around a fireplace
glowing blue,
gave things and a book coded in stone
half symbol of march...
I will research on it
Will let you know. I have lot of banal stuff to do.

Extra seven minutes

The depth of truth intrigue and paradoxical

Dictum of the infinite unknowable
A torch of foam folding social surface

A pillar of liquid that gravity forgot to suck

A transparent mirror. Quintessential harmony which space
time never proscribed

A prosody in vacuum which impregnate itself by the sperm of
curiosity

Unquivering in vagina of 'Prakriti'(Nature Subtle)

Deep in golden hue. The thin. Scarce and subtle in swallow

Dropped like bomb from space in curvature

Sprinkle of hallucination with absolute solidity in
Brownian motion

Glow of time. Eternal. Sky a lie in infinity's curl

Stars separate island built on lightyears
Magic of contortions. Unbroken in swirl
giant miniscule eyes

I shoot up and bring a sac of hollowness and mix with a
bottle of darkness to create alchemical love with flesh as
hue
and it slipped

Here I steal. Create Bluefield, Redfield, Purple field, Silver
field with liquid rainbow. Never vanishes half wonder

A twist in permanence of life non finishing,
gene splitting in desire and harems
code explode

Virtual reality in biological intelligence,
a cranial distribution glow as darkness
shading scales deducing law of smoke imagery

Fresh and sunny. Bright and whimsical

Methods discovered spewed pattern. Repetitions. Laws of
nature. Inventions and inventories

Grand grand clues that capture swathes, ice, water, greens
mountains

Quotidian and gaps. Bright big gaps. Hollowness frees the
will

Fly upwards.... without up or down

Reference frames open and hidden

Measurements invisible as quarks

Down up, Up Down. Top and

Bottom at the fundamental scale

Pure as nothingness

*Twisted as pelvis. Disordered inner law Timeless in event
horizon*

Swashbuckling demystification of endless dot

A beginner's plasticity

Story strings in notations vibrating in geometrical pattern.
Non latticial

All temporary. Sugar salt dissolves in water...we do not.
Success and failure laced water surprised by magic

Ambition drugged one species. First birds showed the way

Mountains and trees trigonometric curiosity

Us struggled with kink. Moved heaven closer in spaceship
Bright and bold. Determination steely

Imagination to beat starbelt, galaxies
cushioned by local cluster

Belief as Graphene. It is progress by smelling failure.
Challenge laugh, crushed and rebuilt around the bent

Symphony grand
repertoire unmeasured playful void
thin ice weather...outsmarted
chained live pushed throb in space

Moon hot and sexy lingerie
velvet night sky
Play neuronal sonata. Bath love in
fire and erotica that smell as Mirabilis Jalapa

Discontinuity stitching silk

Us complex dust in belief

Plan outlast eternity
planet hopping to Mars,
inverse dream bubble. We are we
Infectious........desire fascistic, man eat dog

Trance of liquid dream. Weighed by thickness and foresight.

A lustful journey will become fresh

Seasons wings time. Painted in petals. Nightingale bird's
song. Lyre bird mimicry. In butterflies dazzling colour
Moonlight riverside

Calmness filled with sensuous virility

Around and around encompassing volatile senses that stab
the eye

Diversity always turn to life

Fresh as death

Bold as wind

Half cooked as wisdom

Creativity "Blackhole" in zero gravity.
Impossibility, unconnected, unthought
imagination's limit

That glass is not a glass.

Water is not water.

Love is not love.

*Desire in camouflage by genes and hormones cheat
consciousness*

A naked bed call that sustains sensory memory as
hypothalamus, amygdala web long term attachment with
pain and pleasure centre entwined

Flashes manifold. Recall generated different mood and
shades
Coalesce and breakups

Events shades life that pass as wind keeping memories to
cook emotional recipes with age
For rumination.

Until silence stops sucking oxygen

Brain plays backward for extra seven minutes
After heart and pulse vanishes

That's grace mark of time beyond death.
To produce flashes. What missed and lived. Emotional
film.
Sporadic replay

A token gift of impermanence
losing density beating time

Abhimunya in Kaurav's Chakrbuhya

Sometimes I walk on a
mediumless boulevard
on a zero gravity road with ease

See poems as hanging garden
Rain droplets bonding
with liquid fire
form shiny stars

Smells move upward

Love as windy arrow

Old as dreaming childhood

Music as Satan's trap

God as dark angel

Sagacious talking crap

It encapsulates me
inside a stretched grey wing
that bombard the sensation
with molten glass droplets
and sting

One is always a newcomer
in this reality.

Departed wise
had assembled in a tea joint
planning an uprise

Injecting
soundless words in the soul of
martyrs who had fallen
fighting British

A new revolution underway
I walk in surprise.

See another world
people are melting gold
burning cash to cook novels

A train arrived in unstructured station
laid eggs and then opened wings and
flied away.

the dust gravitate upwards on milky way
pulled the stars as silky blinking sheet
close and tight
night sky vanished

The moon exposed

as rock and stone flying
Sun switched off combustion lost light and rained ice that
fell as dream.

A pair of peacock and peahen cleaning feather to wear
Armani.
A rabbit became carnivorous fighting hyenas to devour
carcass of unknown
origin.

Layers of dreams weaving and ebbing
a psychedelic conundrum....

Between

curvy and straight

satan and divine

failure and glory

cutting and connecting

zero and infinity

illusion and illusion of perception

where electricity is enzyme

creating soup

mind body and consciousness
spinning in a dark chamber
that creates the film

Eighty percent of my blackbox
is water

having half life
of existence
called unknown unknown

Krishna called Arjuna out
from Subhadra's room

Half alighted
Abhimunya started walking in a labyrinth
where sunlight is darkness
entered deep into known unknown
Krishna tiptoed into silence
by intervening
painted known known
thereby
disproved omniscience.

Corpus deliciti

Verrückt, parasite, cheesy, leech,
enemy blood, garbage..Rohingyas,
M word of religion ...all suckers of Bharat Mata.

Came from our divided body and soul
Now....unauthorised "Gushpetis"
All convertees
Enjoying citizen rights ...

All be blood hounded, NPR, NRC, CAA
Be deported. Non – Indian's

Concentration camps, on the vultures sight ...religion of
carrion ...that will make
Auschwitz wonder.
May be I am overdoing it
Pain of partition and loss
twentieth centuries' setback burning

Unfolding drama .. polarization....
votebank call .... shout louder ......

Parasites right
among grand ....Hindus .. ?
Will be barbed, tangled and seperated
No papers, no rights .
Not for killing, but snatching dignity .

Allowed one toilet per thousand
In the distant ten by ten sucker cell
Where darkness squeeze daylight.
Mount of dung scavenger screamed for the zombies
..stateless ..unwashed .

Vibrate, rise "O" mediocrity,
Democracy, last hope,
Power playing judiciary
and configured,

System plotted division
putting people against people

Voice thunder in unison ...
Spiny democracy,
You are the least failed invention
of mankind and now on edge.
Don't disappoint
Hope liquid and glow.

How douse, this blood sucking
Nasty game, continuance of power
Enjoying few,
Fight freely, without violating violence,
Till conscience smell the last breadth.

Lemniscate

Biggest explosion
immeasurable;

Beginning...... begins......
Significance in infinite split,
second, inverse Decillionth more, everything from
undefined Singularity...

Not all metallic yet grouped earth in mould
Air, oxygen, hydrogen, dust...
turns soup into variety,

Water intelligence in shortcuts,
screwing the shell... plants rise,
new faces emerge, life significant less, creative biped,
architecture kisses blue...catch me if you can.. a game of
chicken and egg...unobservable face it's paradox

Drunken days, bloodthirsty rapture,
Emptiness feared for its soul..
Sounds of waterfall, birdsong,
Rabindrasangeet, Haribol....Haribol, death of the
ambushed, the addled remains, carries infinite plots....

Cuddled multitude devours the rest,
Gluttony of sounds headed north..where written on the
wall "No Chance "...virginity looted in silent heist...

Here Sun does not know what moon witnessed, neutron
star bimboed,
universe awed, in a spec space thawed
progression....
split looted everything
a bunch of mortals plotted all....

Now time charting course and carve matter and space on
the roll...

Don't be fearful the belly yells, I am still naked, wild,
molten and spinning, can spew matter, but like them I
cannot grow in geometric progression@open.com

Broken Mirror-19th April 2020

Garbage less visible.
No broken bridges or house, no sound blast, no siren, no
burning smell of flesh,
no blood spilled open .....
It cannot be a war.

Fear all around
Human rubble to be cleared from hospitals, without
victory..
there is no surrender.

Once it was a equalizer.
Ramesses V succumbed with thousands ordinary in small
pox 1142 B.C.
Vaccine came 1796 A.D.
Now...Rich...can postpone death like Alien gods.

New hell, cleansing...elderly, ethnic minorities....and as it
does best..the poor...its ruthless, without border.

Cities ghost town, enemy invisible...
milling bodybags with precision...without bullet.

Speeding military trucks, funeral cars loaded, heading
massgrave..dumping untouchables..no teardrops.

Human fearing human....Masked.

Kiss...electronic, feeling contactless.
Mother seeing son on the net.
Touch...is death...defy law of life.

Without us, nature is singing...
trees bloom, birds, animals reclaimed their city rights.

Rich...counting loss of profit. Others begging food,
walking thousand miles back, slaughtered by train, hunger
and exhaustion.

One little girl...standing alone
lost parents, confused
clueless of the loss...
photogenic...missing shooter.

The grasses, knows it all, old smell of human blood and
flesh after every ravage.
Political garbage.. untrammelled.

Blood, oxygen, hunger, bodybags
Upside down....

Up cloud....holding souls
as raindrops
to wash....pain someday.

Form

Everything I hear
fractional narrative

Everything I see
a..trailer

Everything I smell
a local veil

when dream
scattered..   unphrased....

event appear and vanishes
when I say, gap remains
between thinking and saying
time hollowed
meaning partial
what said... bit surreal
what unsaid...a fountain.

Between silence and words
a painting emerges
that cannot be painted.....
an abstract...borderless

it is a discontinuity, a gap
world without physical form
no meaning only experience
between I and me...
it floats....undefined......

The shadow that brighten the soil

Walking through centuries .....

MYTH older than history
A connection of previous birth
with same shops and stacks
like unrepaired pillars of bridge....

College resembles museum, university
playhouse, fading faces jumps from ponds..as fishes, the slippery
faces in artery of college street
Caught the flash of special face
a girl fresh as dew on black rose at dawn.

Noticed Manikda'r dokan where time stuck..... to have a
glance
Before entering the Grand Hall.

Spirit of giants hover...
Everest of Bengali pride....
Shine in pitch dark
Assemble at Indian Coffee House...
Bodiless...

Want to hear them by becoming silence.

A large wave hit me with rusty smell
from the shop...

Time lost itself
Lifted and amazed

A Book, wordless, but filled with sentence...
No language, history holding time
An aura gleaming
unopened for ages

It's bindings shows previous owner taste.

Aristocrat, through and through
Like my ignorance
Lived with it, wrote events with memory.

*Painted the pages from inside with brushes that glow as
revolution.*

The second page....history of Time
A house.... complex characters played in the rough sea,

*A invisible hull glows from the boundary with fifteen sails in
cyclone
gilded page cannot hold.*

The third page mysterious as dark energy
with three ladies wearing saree, one girl in silk frock
dancing in a old Irish tune that memory instantly did not
serve.....

But smell of jealousy, adultery, murder, corruption and
crosscurrents of failed ambitions
Sketched in every blank page

Web hanging in mirror and they are real.
Rest of the pages unwalked.

Inside every page unrest dwell in the walls but ceilings and
floor witness memories.

In this overgrown castle I am the uninvited.

This wordless book is a ocean of turmoil
Coated in snowflake

House of conflict from where every characters wanted to
escape,
None succeed..
I sensed it.

Both joy and sorrow from the serenity of cold night beside
a stilly lake...to "Amphan" twister visible through the lens
of first dew on that black rose...
The face flashes again
Evening sun, set the tune to orange

I slowly closed fourth page as load levelled with blank
sight
Walked towards the Square to see the
water pool.

Upon entering
saw liquid glass shining in dusk
A window to the heaven stored to fate..earth

History on each drops hold eternity
Befriended sky and the liquid silvery mirage speaks on the
tip....
Foams whispers and crashes..

Came out... reached the grand house
Ordered a cup...

Sits are filled to the corner
Faces known but some names unfigured
Speaking voiceless with clear accent

Some shadows clear as mirror
I overheard silent conversation of the invisibles.

Literature must invent new language,
More experimental aesthetics, new metaphors, new vistas

Sense and nonsense
must walk in creation

Paint the unpaintable...

using sounds...as brush

space borderless canvas

where silence of choice .....

mixes the colour of sounds

with inner eye

post- modernism in coded post language form

a cocktail of feeling....

connects wireless to the souls.....

Art is a private experience
Reader and writer fuses as one.

Experience... inexplicable.

Must float between unconscious and ecstasy where few can travel.

Sculptor

Standing still where
light and darkness collide
time motionless...
some thoughts...

Dream...
burst through the chasm
enter my eyes, nerves,
veins, tissues and scatters....
in search of the source....

the fountain.... of OBSESSION
the smell, the fire, the curves
the rose...which turn blood
when you are near
in a saree...

that bust, navel, hair, eye and waist
in choreography
like daisy in summer
evening breeze...
undeciphered smile
make epic forgot...

the fantasy in the
phantom's illusion..

who made you
how could he let go !
for mere mortals...
must be blind.....
a mad sculptor.....?

The heart of the matter

Practice, practice
more and more.....

The guru repeats
and the Raag "Deepak" Bilwal Thaat
is not easy to master.

She repeats and repeats
each arohan and abrohan
twist and turns every slow movements
perfection a mirage.

Slowly she gains the movement's fluctuations under
control and errors
recedes.

A guru I met
gave this example

Learn to detach
learn to lose
learn to be non materialistic
It's easier...on surface
Very hard to practice
It's art, takes time to master

And I felt it.

I lost lakhs in stockmarket
that's a game of bets....statistical
with occasional bias

I lost friends
I lost insurance cover
I lost first love
I left job and lost income
Lost seven kilos
Lost umbrella, doorkeys bunch,
believed one old man who made profit
by selling mangos in Corona times
I lend him six hundred rupees
and he vanished from the spot.

These losses are minor waves
and I learnt loosing a bit many times

Then a day came I lost half of my soul.
25th April 2017 my mother left of septicaemia.
Following year father followed.

The pain and loss unbearable
I gave her a pricey red and goldensilk saree
Asked her to wear in Durgapuja.
She said....marry first
on that day
I will wear it.

Sisters covered her body with that saree
pushed inside electric chamber

She spoke with a pasted eye in red vermilion tip " don't I
look like a bride and a caring mom " as family shrank....

Three years hence
grief alive but I can write now.
Time is slow ointment
don't work smoothly.

We lose small things everyday
often uncared
Big losses are always emotional

Four pillars hold us throughout.

First... the day body will stop working
Then you will leave all assets for which
you worked throughout life.
Finally no one....no one will be with
you in this journey including wife or son.

But only soul..as they say...which
we never considered....may be friend

Loss is not art...
A mind which never bothers losses
is an artist
Learning to take losses is never going
to be a disaster.
Life is a minus sign with positive
bubbles and flashes
Grinding prepares a man to master
this art

All of us can be a artist..
It's already exist inside
We can harness it
It will set it's course
make life easy for oneself

Will set us free....

The Day Next

I was wandering, aimlessly
in the morning next, locally to see nature
against nature, the fury....first hand.

whimsical strides of the few in
waterlogged roads, curious residents, silence and sounds of
occasional electrical cutters, used by policemen, cutting
logs..of blocked roads, lanes and bye lanes...I did not
imagine my city with green leaves in stroves, mango,
banyan all face down each other on the washed muddy grey
pitch..ever in my imagination...Shyambazar to southern
avenue and chetla any road in between, the silent cries of
the uprooted...the death pain everyone feeling as someone
of their own in accident are up in the air .

Two beautiful pair, Krishnachura and Radhachura beneath
my floor..down facing each other saying their final
goodbye's after fifty years of togetherness creating sea of
dead flower of red and yellow in each season with final
kisses..slowly in a downdrift and four pair of crows
constantly crying for the lost nest with tiny kids nowhere
in sight. The pain is palpable as they lost shelter and
families and asking every passer by to help find their
babies.....
My parents faced the same...when they were uprooted from
Bangladesh during partition...

The emotional loss are universal, the occasional burst of electric horn brings back normalcy to senses as few bikes and cars running over countless fallen leaves, branches, stems random orientation and carefully bypassing fearing accidents...this time nature revenged against big trees as it may seem that trees were the target thousands upon thousands ...what happened in Sunderban, Hathia...Kolkata alike..recognizing park street is tough and Bhwanipur, north Calcutta...most huts decimated....small room in ground floor filled to the waist.

The City of Joy is in tatters...as there is silence, disbelief and dismay all around ..the high risers were also not spared...broken window panes, littered glasses and stems on their cars..crashed.

There is no scale to measure pain and our ears cannot hear the cry of the banyan tree in Alipore road crossing who was a friend of my grandfather and a family friend and still love me as grandchild...all its doing is its leaves are staring at me saying that it still loves me...and slowly gravity and sun sucking the links of the branch and as it falls on the grey muddy pitch it said me a final goodbye.

Spit

Do we kiss the lips,
skin, tissue, skeleton,
the soul, or
unknowable ?

Rain or sun put imprint like our sight,
Drops of light, cold and glow on the
cable, against wheels scratching pitch.

Sensual wind cooking for clues,
Spiritual wild beneath the silk
ugly surprise.

Crows ponder in uncanny silence,
Mirror and water, are shady characters,
One servant of light, other mix almost everywhere.

Theories of Mind...
Figure...Anticipation, ..

Character....smells power,
Blood spilled
Spit filled the road, arrowed to heart
carries venom ...everywhere.

God...seems hiding
Between fear and the cunning
Thousands of years.

Cloud and I

I was dreaming...flying beside
a piece of lonely cloud..
I asked....where others ?
she laughed, I am virgin...
I said, down there we have
life...vibrating, miracles, flowers,
birds, sea, mountain...but here nothing.

she laughed, yes we are black and grey
but have you seen the evening, when
sun turn red and make us play ?
we make earth glow as heaven...what sun
say...
when we drizzle in the hot summer you bath, when fall as
snow, make your heart wild and play, rainy season... we
make you lush, even desert green, life sings.

I said, I have three wishes...
fly like you and see the blue earth on the wings, second,
reborn like you and finally free of form, desire, hatred,
jealousy, blood, killing born out of greed and power...and
filling field which will produce land of gold below...

I asked her what are your wishes ?
without a second she said one, to rain on the sun, to soothe
him of the rage and fill him with the music, beauty
rhythm and song of me...the falling rain.

Tango

I stole few drops of crystal
from the lightning...and bead
from the sunset,
I want to weave the star with coral
necklace...to an undressing jingo of the
naked soul.

Justice for the grasses,
that misses the moon....

The wine from human blood
I want to share with the darkness, that
Repair in silence, the Cold heart....
what light fails to do later
or soon.....

The edge of isolation, desire unfurl in the night...the sassy
time fire the senses, kisses the rainbow of surprise,
sprinkle lava,
into liquid delight...

Political doctrine, moral hazard, ethical acts whirls by the
human drain in the night washroom....

Life's slugfest, takes the rest.....
and drama of neurons
emerges from the tissue's shadow....

kicks the blood and testosterone
to play with the smell of estrogen
and sweat, a carnal affair,
Blast inside naked skull....
creating Tango....by the atoms in
nervy mating ball.

Black Paradise

I was looking for paradise

....Which one among
millions, billions of stars ...
infinity....confounded.. want a piece
to bring in my room...my city
where my people are called seasonal labourer...diseased,
shunted...without relief.

I hold a piece of cloth from Puri Jagganath...that magical
touch, carrying blessings of paradise.

I kept it in pocket and moved around not to be touched by
evil, and every work, I hold that Midas of Paradise in my
forehead.

One friend's mother told....never loose, evil fear this
magical wand...so I kept it
beside my pillow night after night.

Some night...I want to smell moonlight, at dawn, wear
morning mist, a sneaky led street lamp sharp knive flashed
to steal...

Flicker of glance, looked at it with awe, and fell asleep...
...a patch of earthly wind wings it through my window .....
in silence,

blessings in the drain....
became bedfellows of waste......
infinity now terrestrial and finite,
blackness rain.

Heaven mixed dirt, dust, air and drain....
in earth, now whites are blacks
and blacks are lives
paradise shakened
No.....surprise.

Sapiens born colored ....
Differences cultivated
Over and Over again...

From dust and death
Back to Breath
Till Justice embrace

Blacks will rise
and rise
and rise.......

Bloods and fight
make sapiens
equal....
in every right

Utopia..

A moving cradle's cry

Earth...
A piece of it..
My mother when conceived me
she ate whatever little
father brought....

I saw shiny rays that earth received
free..
All living beings.....Accumulate

The big forest, the dwindling decadence
and the geese that travelled continents
and lives..
all be ....Entropied....

The Randomness is Rhythm
Rhythm is order between chaos and breakups

Families form without shelter, food,
struggle in sun and rain
beneath my veranda in footpath.

Yet generation lives on drug, crime, promiscuity, violence
Love flourishes like flowers unseen
on stones
parasites grow,
again new families form...sporadic grasses in Sahara rain.

Divinity is mystery romanticised.

Beauty polishes the soul
open the door temporal
and ask to look at hindsight
what is lost....
And catching the art difficult
as no one want's to die.

The thrill of visual sensation
when she standing naked
or change attire in season
dazzle with colours and fecundity
I am awed, with explosion of primitive
instinct.
untouched still....

The "Amphan" a destruction,
a disordered rhythm, cleaned it's bowel
now regrowing new greens, people
where others perished.....

She don't keep accounts,
profit and losses...absent
her book a chronicle, imaged motion
in discontinuity....billions of years

Careless yet heartbroken saw
millions of her child perished.

I am a dot in this wider scale
Beyond twelve notes.......SHE acts

We don't have infra or ultra sensors ....
the audible, visible....miniscule
draw big inferences in half dark

Hear silence in her composition
Like seeds defy gravity
break her shell and grow,
waterfall spinning music
flowers, fruits
bees, birds butterflies....so many notes
of infinite wonder....

The dead flowers return to her
to her cradle
She silently whispers
wind sings
Aria...
of sadness, grief and ecstasy.

The earth... mother
cradle meets grave...
gives everyone..
takes nothing
her days redlined like all
with the sun....oneday

Sometimes we are butterflies
dance from joy to joy
death....dances soundless
shadowless..beside...

we blossom to blossom
moment will meet
miss the sunrise.

She cries in her soul
shed....seasons
Bleeds within...

No one to share pain
as she weeps for us
when a child is lost.....

what we call life
is her another vein

her pain seen in melted ice
fallen leaves, carcass, genocide
,Tsunamis or her own
madness flashes in quakes,
lightning that kill innocents, us kill
countless colonies of beehives
burned for nectar
We cannot know the art of producing
nectar...and bees know it.

She made every species unique
in a circle of fragmentation
leading to omission.

Like her fertility uninterrupted
amid holocaust and pain
Blood loss by the veins

deeply wounded
everytime a life stops
she looses part of her soul......

Hypothesis

It's everywhere
seas rivers tributaries pond
in your drain, body brain
Its hidden beneath the shell

Sun the magician takes up
Earth pulls music back
the falling...... rain.

The tiny life where it acts
in every tributaries, veins where
it write algorithm that carries
the sunlight in seed gene
to run the code and play
that's us..lives

I often walk that path
Molecules hard at work like labourers
of pharaoh
build child that hides time as Alap in Dhrupad
and Jhad transform root to myriad
branches limbs
Alchemist's hew in silence
colour the petals.. wind water light gene painted by
invisible brush
fragrance flies in the mist
angel's song

Scores grow unnoticed
Flowers fruits bees wasps butterflies
bats know all
hundreds of miles away
they get the call

Patience are fruits of time
I travel forward and backward motionless
under the symphony of double triplet

Light water gene
Distance heat and cold
Invisible brush busy....
painting nature
the miracle unfold

I often here their dance see their rhythm
and pang of separation

they know they are linked with a
umbilical chord
slowly goes up
comes down

Sweet sweet sounds of life
in birdsong animal calls
chase of cheetah
chant of sadhus
beneath beehives

The dancing drops of crystals
in my ears

Adagio...... of falling rain.

Walking in the Veins

Eyes are lakes
Joy brings rain, it's flooded.
Trees are clouds in this mirror
Creates waterpaint in a leather cover
Horizon singing tenor smelled by pupil.

Distance vanishes
Bats are flying low on sonar
The city is thinner, lost fat
Cautious as the invisible
Human are less jerk....

Silence is eating time

Square meals appear round

The parables of the gods are stones

People are offering less

Cartoons are not arranging more.

This summer patience untested
Showers timed the door.

Heat drunk by the city walls
Cars plying at no destination

Jams are memories...
choked city on tour.

Life in vaccine's shadow
Slope of time is still zero
Peace prevails in routine island
Free breathing allowed...only at mountain top and home.

I see the future in crystal ball that
made of iron kaleidoscope revolves
about its axis.

Indoors are now outdoors
Family faces are distinct contours
Like Meer cats....watchful,
discover more in walled tour.

As garden find wind and flowers,
No eye catchers strands,

Seeds and petals in sorrow
falling on fallowed soil becoming
unnoticed.

There are mistakes in distance
Loneliness gulped silence

It is wonderful to hear heartbeats
among the few walking......

*Shadows appear real in darkness
that search partners.*

I see sunshine deep in the night ....

*Kolkata always a song and poetry,
is void, lost shimmering verve
and veins are dry.*

*The city's soul left home without
giving notice, address and time.*

Darkness in walking Liquid

No, it is not about the boundary
Sun faded in the edge of Neptune,
No it is not about the scandal.... politician or celebrity.
No, not about the suffering of the ordinary, or
Corrupt power, endless pain of children in Syria and
Yemen.
O' yes, it is not about Corona virus,
or mine or yours dreams and reality that
ogres series of philosophy starting from
Greek enlightenments to modernism.

It's about material you ; ninety nine point ninety nine
percent vacuum...the earth, moon, sun and all the
stars...everything.
You are space.

With point zero zero zero one percent
We are we..
Scientist from Russia found in permafrost, Arctic where
two worms one aged 41700 years and another 32000 years
started moving and eating
They are healthy

Life...laughs at philosophy, religion

Transience in solidity
anchors in chaos, ripped knowledge
confidence quarantined

Here, thoughts are glasses.
Infinity bleeds infinity.

Darkness is gleaming light, hangs as Damocles sword on
omniscience.

Death is leaf, painted in canvas
Turns brain fog to a forest

Where we stand in the mist
Surrounded by edge of
Slippery existence

Basic harpooned millennia
Shoot surprises beyond time.

A vagabond scribbler

Who claims that writing
is all about passion..
Being unworthy myself,
at best a scribbler
oblique confession a virtue
I barf my anguish or absurdity.

The reference point a meadow
drinking gallons,
from the perilous sun
where darkness meets
the mate, filled dotted mysteries
an epiphany, of silence,
drum beats that caress the skin,
One fire awaits another,
to dye our rush...Dopamine.

An incessant burst of whirring...
a move of stallions in skinfield,
cells dance, and dark room
running wilder than Kenya,

Dearest....as fireplace we become,
the music fills...and our
naked work justify life..

Our LOVE,
a miracle....add one more layer
of mystery.....in absurd infinity of
lifelessness.

Soul

I look in the mirror everyday
to see through... inside
in search of... soul...
I always return empty handed...

I see the sweeper, the fruit seller,
the man, who pulled ashes of my mother still red on fire
through back a hole the
crematorium,
Saw baby
Crying on the footpath....with flies sucking runny nose, and
open mouth... naked

Cut the mundane out ..The guru teaches
Search Spiritual Unity inside you...
Breath control...watch..in silence ..
I discovered a poor seeker.

I see struggle in the cut of a uprooted tree wanting to
sprout again...

the baby crow fall from the nest and all the community
shout together to signal danger of their own....to help see it
another day,
I see the mother rat pickup left over food of my lunch and
rush towards her hole to feed hungry pups.

The window views are remarkably lazy,
occasionally bring surprises...the things I never read in
poetry...

I look for higher morals....fail again.

I watch curiously introvert's inner world...the autist, whose
mysterious creation... a wonder ..

The old beggar with white feather
lost strength to ask alms nobody cares to watch in the
corner
at Rashbehari crossing
A silent awe receiving a ten rupee note unfigured...a weak
hand trembling up
Blessed me....

In chicken's death cry, blood and mass, we seek
protein...free to kill
In Kalighat, ask everything from goddess, not see people
unfed for days lying outside ..soul untraceable .....

Often it meet senses,
childhood friend, momentary rapture, memories flood,
Kanchenjunga's golden awe, flashes of first love......

In line of duties...business and politics serial lies, bigotry,
racism, murder, jealousy ethnic cleansing, it is on tour.

We arrive improvised.....No Repetition
each moment in transience.
Wonder pops, in smaller daily grudging.

Days don't copy...context and content changes...every
morning, reborn from slumber.... in a new dream.

Each life...different
Rose or rock
surprise flashes...in the ordinary.
So many stories
Vast ocean...

Life and Soul never fuses...like two water drops........

Smoke and Glow

Shadows black and bleak
through twisted veins
trigger the dots of hope
carries flight of the river
rises in the mist and cloud
dashing the abyss of heat
enlighten the sun
to smell cold in silence
drench in wonder rain....

With torch of life
wings flying high
from the nest in stone
between red and grey
the spirit of time
dropped rainbow

Slowly sucked lightning
in thick of confusion
with the tender hands
firmly as snow.....

trapped between
waves and moon
the silky
vortex rise
and rise
and rise
untill the peak
of obscure clarity...
glow..
that nothing... I know.

Love without a cut

You love me
can do anything
first blush, sensual eyes, champagne overflows, candlelight
dinner.....

Souls flood emotions
the dried rose petal in the vase
facing death....smiling....

The countless coffin of broken vows
shredded timelapse image
the quagmire of oxytocin
dances on the narrowed bye lane of veins...oblivious of the
future.

Life beats inside egg...
small trees kiss rain, sun.. grow,
metamorphosed caterpillar stun everyone and pollinate.....
semi naked mother with empty bellies begging, raises her
future with drops from dried breast..

Often, tall trees fall
and the forest lose height.
Few big star explodes, supernova
become space dust.

The moon knows everything
create illusion for the hearts to sing...
achieve the goal of the heaven
to touch possibility....of the impossible
immortality....in love....

Life pulls souls together
howsoever brief, create magic...till the
invisible door open, the golden moments shine..in memory
wine.

As much as you got....cannot be undone.

The journey began from Crag

Counting seconds,
shuffling high turnover memories
near the crag.
Mind is heavier than sun.

Faint vibrations of glow warm
rekindled hope

Below a void
shoot's enigma of brazen dark

Silent voices clutter
Time halted.

The city leds and red signals
hazily creating synchronous que
Like thrombocytes in fat clump.

No one knows, a spirit surrendered.
Somewhere a violin sonata create web
of music piece that is a cold light.

Under the base a banyan tree, third eye
of Shiva Linga looking as a Cyclop
And counting.

Somehow the forty third storey jump is

aborted half way.
The serotonin as cobblestones fused
depressive episode .

There he sat for hours with lightning flashes in Amygdala .
Neurons of prefrontal cortex overpowered
Thought artery opened.

He knew the trip would have been short.

Now the mind gliding on the ice
The race of the heart staggered
slopey downward
Long deep breadth...

Aboard clusters of unhooked memories.
You don't have to die
An inner call.
The darkness that thud heart
on a temporary retreat..

Scared frigid, without energy
completed unknown steps down
stood in front road

Removed spear from the soul
Looked up a moment
where clasped like a nail
Pulse returned from
abyss precipice.

Stopped a cab
got inside and lost into the darkness
of throbbing led.

My dream cracked, a car overturned
beside my room.
Psychiatrist explored but stuttered figured depression
untraceable...

Yet REM sleep short circuits depth
often, shoots this colourless record

And at noon
I walk in the dark.....
miles in horizon
destination nowhere........

Classified 2019

A forgotten chapter
All those who counted on you
ashed away.
For those remained, will unlearn
you, replaced by new flame.

Tired mind will walk the shadows
as moon's path erase the calendar days
the led and glasses count the
routine.

Inevitable melancholic journey sounds
like worn out long play records
carrying same tune....
No one remembers you... four face,
personality...one for the world, one for family, one for the
self and last your dead dreams you knew was in your grip
but missed and the alter ego sues.

I see the vacant bed where moonlight
skimmed, my dear souls.. parents..dark
skull inside flashes the lullabies....
And the music plays...
I lift my head in the night sky...
the gift that was taken away..

Miracles are stories of time

I have crossed that age,
Looking up, watching the
dark delight ....
Thus far, privileged to see the wonder
the dotted vibrations in extension
It's a gift ..a true gift....I realise
it could be otherwise.

Shadows

Mystery, infinity and more mystery
in your neuron... there is no entry
the Game of twisted Shadows... and loving rhyme
The smell of time... the fear of love
the sound of Shadows... the music of oxygen
the echoes of silence...the shadows of fear
the dance of death...
Ha ha ha....

Twisted shadows, colourful shadows
screams the life of the gone
vaginas...stopped bleeding and euphoric
oozes life... from a pair of gene that stuck on
Shadows of the lost... smiles gleefully
as they pass on.

Darkness gives colour and soup.. to the skeleton
that feeds... the hungry souls... wait for life
Dance of Shadows like the Moon's camouflage
a dark stone on the run...reflects glow in fun
secretly conceals shadow
beneath the light... of the sun

Billions of lives... invisible souls
dances in the darkness... nothingness grind
Desires of mind... shadows of the wind
weaving of the blind...

remained mystery forever...
Illusion of a kind...

Shadows... shadows of darkness
mocks the rainbow in the light
A hole in The Shadow by a wandering Photon
splits darkness into melody white
Shadows burst... in the vastness... with inaudible cry
laughter of the hope fades...before a genuine try

Greed... fucking greed, desires and passion burn
on the planet earth...
Tears of shadow.... sparkle in the darkness
create eternal delight... raises heaven's fun

Poetry

what is it?
what it has to be?
It has history of sonnet, rhyme, lyric, meter, narrative, free
verse...
banal unstructured form...

Yet it is undefined..
words, expressions, perceptions, emotions, reality ..inner,
outer life, nature, poverty, society, war, spirituality,
inequality, marginalized
anything...everything its fodder......

still nobody knows its core...
even poets unsure...

few read..fewer understand
abstractions galore..
can earn noble prizes..
for advancement of literature, new
poetic form, style, innovation,
excellence, critical acclamation...
But still.... what is it?

aesthetics...bigger than ethics and moral, poetry should
have it..

People living beside Tollynala....the drain

where dengue, corona, malaria and smell of burning rotten
flesh, fall as ashes in leaky plastic shades of Jhupri, on
their new born, face, milk..no one complain... God and
society has abandoned....life goes...on.

There, a boy singing Arijit flashes talent in the void....
zenith, nadir meaningless.

Is it song or poetry..? Epiphany....not so....
But poets...often imagine ..and express.

People of colour.....discrimination
unemployment, impoverished, struggle, torture...death...
where aesthetics...fit..?
open question......

Use...of
local slangs...unbarred....

Still cannot compromise aesthetics..
But still what is poetry?

Target government policies, criticize,
Write...facts ..could face jail..
Politicians fearful....of mass sway.....

But it's not for the poetic art,
fear of poet's influence...on a issue

Surprise still, it does not answer the question ! ! !

unanswerable...harmony, abstraction
have doubts....even masters.

For me it rises from the ashes, rubbles, genocide, racism,
religious persecution, fundamentalism and human private
condition as pain, suffering, loneliness and love.

For lovers who love to ride,
it's not entertainment
It rises above specific gravity of words

Knock ......unknown corners
Beyond meaning,
Floats somewhere in the unconscious consciousness.